D0300851

This book
belongs to

....

Cuddle's Fan Pages

Here's what other children have to say about their favourite kitten and her first adventure!

"I loved the part where the kitten kept disappearing. This was a fun story and made me laugh." Abby, age 6

"I think Cuddle is very helpful. It's nice that the girls made friends with each other. I liked Cleo the cat – she is cheeky. It is a bit funny to have a big party for a cat, but nice." Lucina, age 5

"I loved it and I love Cuddle. My favourite bit was the kitten makeover. I liked learning about pyramids. I wish I had a toy Cuddle." Caitlin, age 7

"I really liked Olivia and Grace and loved it when they got lost in the pyramid. I would love a kitten like Cuddle." Piper, age 7

"I like Cuddle, as her friends Olivia and Grace are seven like me. I like it best when Cuddle is cheeky and does her magic. My favourite part of the book is when they describe the magical pyramid; also the bits when they find the Pharaoh's missing kitten." Daisy, age 7

Magical Friends

Other books about
Cuddle the Cutest Kitten:

Superstar Dreams
Princess Party Sleepover
School of Spells

Cuddle
★ the cutest kitten ★

Magical Friends

by Hayley Daze
Illustrated by Ann Kronheimer
Cover illustrated by Amanda Gulliver

A catalogue record for this book is available from the British Library

Published by Ladybird Books Ltd
A Penguin Company
Penguin Books Ltd., 80 Strand, London WC2R 0RL, UK
Penguin Books Australia Ltd., Camberwell, Victoria, Australia
Penguin Group (NZ) 67 Apollo Drive, Rosedale,
North Shore 0632, New Zealand

001 – 10 9 8 7 6 5 4 3 2 1
Series created by Working Partners Limited, London WC1X 9HH
Text © Working Partners Ltd MMXI
Cover illustration © Working Partners Ltd MMXI
Interior illustrations © Ladybird Books Ltd MMXI

Special thanks to Elizabeth Galloway

ISBN: 978-1-40930-850-8
Printed in England

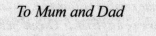

To Mum and Dad

Cuddle the kitten has black-and-white fur,
A cute crooked tail, and a very loud purr.
Her two best friends, Olivia and Grace,
Know Cuddle's world is a special place!

Just give her a cuddle, then everything spins;
A twitch of her whiskers, and magic begins!
So if you see a sunbeam, and hear Cuddle's bell,
You can join in the adventures as well!

Contents

Contents

Chapter One
The Magic of Friendship

As if by magic, a grinning face framed by springy brown curls popped up above Grace's garden fence. Then, in a flash, it was gone. Grace rubbed her eyes. Maybe she was so lonely she was making up imaginary friends.

The curly head appeared again, bobbing along the fence. Two hands gripped the top of the wooden slats and then the smiling face looked over.

"I'm Olivia," the curly-haired girl
said. "My mum says you're our new
neighbour."

"Hi," Grace replied. "I'm Grace."
Her smile was as bright as her shiny
blonde hair.

Olivia stood on tiptoes and peered further over the fence. Grace's garden had a sandpit, a bench, and a vegetable patch filled with juicy tomatoes and stringy beans. But Olivia was staring at a triangular pile of boxes in the middle of the lawn.

"Nice pyramid," she said.

"Oh – thanks," Grace replied. "Those are the removal boxes Mum and Dad have unpacked."

She grabbed a box and placed it on the top of the pyramid. "I used to live on a farm. It's funny seeing so many tall buildings around here, so I thought I'd make one myself!"

The sky above them darkened as grey clouds glided across the sun.

"Is it always cloudy in Catterton?" Grace asked.

Olivia nodded. "Pretty much. But don't worry, it doesn't mean we can't have fun. We can play dressing up indoors or chase rainbows in the garden. The best thing about living here is there's always someone to play with." She smiled. "You just have to know where to look."

Olivia dropped down behind the fence, out of sight. Grace jumped as high as her trainers would take her, but it looked like Olivia's back garden was empty. She had vanished.

"Close your eyes," Olivia called.

Grace squeezed her eyes tightly shut.

"Ta-dah!" Olivia said. Grace's eyes snapped open. Olivia was standing right in front of her.

"How did you do that?" Grace asked. "It's like magic!"

Olivia's curls bounced as she shook her head. "It's not magic," she said, taking Grace's hand. "But it can be our secret!"

Olivia showed her a section of the fence that was partly hidden by a rose bush. One of the wooden panels was hanging loose at the bottom. Olivia pulled it so it swung upwards,

making a gap just big enough to
squeeze through.

"It's like a giant cat flap," Grace
said as she peeked into Olivia's
garden.

Olivia laughed. "You're right! Miss
Nancy, the old lady who used to live
in your house, had seven cats. We
made the flap in the fence so I could

come and play with them."

Grace's mouth fell open.

"Seven cats?"

"I wish I could have just one," Olivia sighed, "but my dad's allergic to them. He used to start sneezing if he even looked at one of Miss Nancy's cats."

"I can't have one either," Grace said. "I've got a new baby brother. Mum says I have to wait until he's older."

Olivia sat down on the bench, her shoulders slumped. The garden felt empty without Miss Nancy's cats.

"What should we do now?" she asked her new friend.

"I know! Let's see how far we can

climb up that tree." Grace pointed
to the apple tree at the foot of
the garden.

Olivia straightened her spotless denim skirt. "I'm not really dressed for climbing," she said. "But we could play movie star makeover. I'm going to be an actress one day, so I've got everything we need."

She opened the sequinned bag that was always slung across her shoulder and took out a hairbrush and some sparkly hair grips.

A sudden burst of brightness made both girls shield their eyes. The grey clouds drifted apart and a sunbeam shone down on to Grace's garden. It showered the cardboard pyramid with sparkling golden light.

Jingle jangle jingle.

"Did you hear that?" Grace asked.

"It sounded like a bell."

"Look!" Olivia shouted and pointed to Grace's cardboard tower. Sitting at the top of the pyramid, her eyes narrowed in the sunlight, was the cutest kitten either of the girls had ever seen.

Chapter Two
The Jingle-Jangle Bell

The kitten's fur was white, with one black ear and what looked like black socks on her two front paws. Her tail had a black tip and a curly kink – like a fuzzy pipe-cleaner.

Her pink tongue flicked in and out as she washed her paw.

She turned her green eyes towards the girls and gave a loud "Miaow!".

Then the tiny cat bounded down the pile of boxes and on to the grass. She was small enough to fit inside Olivia's bag. The girls knelt beside her, and the kitten stretched her head towards them.

"She wants to say hello," Grace said. She leant down so she could bump heads with the kitten.

Olivia did the same and the kitten rubbed against her cheek.

"Your whiskers tickle," she said.

Grace gave the kitten a stroke, from the tip of her pink nose to the curly kink in her tail. The kitten flopped on to her back, showing her fluffy white tummy.

There was a *jingle jangle* as she rolled about, and the girls saw a tiny silver bell under her chin. It was attached to a sparkly pink collar.

"Miss Nancy's cats had name tags with her phone number on," Olivia remembered. "Let's see who you

31

belong to." She felt all around the kitten's collar, but there was nothing on it except the bell.

Grace tickled the kitten's tummy. The little cat gave her fingers a lick, then stretched her paws up in the air.

"Look, she wants a cuddle," Grace said.

Olivia rubbed the velvety tip of the kitten's nose.

"Cuddle," she said thoughtfully. "You know, she likes being stroked

and tickled. Cuddle is the perfect
name for her."

The kitten gave a "Miaow!" as if
she agreed.

Grace laughed. "Cuddle it is."

With a flick of her tail, Cuddle
rolled on to her tummy. She crouched
low to the ground, looking up at the
girls.

"What is it, Cuddle?" Olivia asked.
"Do you want to play?"

Cuddle bounded back over to the
cardboard pyramid. She scampered
round it, her bell jingling, then
hopped on to one of the boxes. The
pyramid wobbled as she jumped from
box to box, right to the top.

"Oh no," said Grace. "It's going to collapse!"

Just as the pyramid tumbled to the ground, Cuddle sprang through the air and landed safely in Olivia's arms.

"You crazy kitten," Olivia said, cradling her. Grace stroked Cuddle's silky ears.

Purrrrrrrrr, went Cuddle.

Olivia wriggled. She felt ticklish all over. "Do you feel ... tingly?" she asked Grace.

Grace nodded.

The girls started to giggle. Cuddle purred even louder and the tickling sensation grew stronger and stronger. The garden became a blur of greens and browns. The girls were laughing so much that both of them closed their eyes, and the world disappeared around them . . .

Chapter Three
Sandy Surprise

Grace wondered if she was in bed. Maybe she was dreaming about a new friend and a cute kitten. She was lying down, covered in something warm. It didn't feel like her soft duvet, though – it was grainy, and she could move her fingers through it. She opened her eyes and gasped. "Sand!"

The mound of sand next to her

stirred and Olivia sat up, shaking the grains from her curls.

"This is one of your magic tricks, isn't it – like the thing you did with the fence?" Grace asked, feeling silly. "You've made us appear in the sandpit."

But Olivia's eyes were wide with astonishment. "Grace," she said slowly, "we're not in your garden any more."

Instead of wooden fences and big brick buildings, Olivia and Grace were surrounded by sand – lots and lots of sand – dotted with palm trees. The sky was deep blue and the air shimmered with heat. Cuddle

was a few paces away, shaking sand
from her black-and-white fur. She
miaowed in greeting as the girls ran
over to her.

"Was it you, Cuddle? Did you bring us here?" Grace asked. She remembered the tickling sensation and the kitten's loud purr before she'd closed her eyes.

Cuddle rubbed against Grace's leg. She flicked her crooked tail and leapt into Grace's arms. Her eyes narrowed as if she knew a secret.

"It's like she's saying yes," Olivia said, scratching Cuddle under her furry chin.

"A magic kitten," Grace exclaimed. "That's amazing!"

Olivia pointed into the distance. "And so is that."

Grace turned to look. Towering in

front of them was a gigantic pyramid. Its smooth sides were made from white stone that gleamed in the sunlight. Crouched beside it was an enormous statue with a human head and a lion's body, its front paws stretched out.

Grace couldn't believe her eyes. "A real pyramid," she said. "And what kind of creature is that statue?"

"A sphinx," Olivia said. "I saw it in a film once – *Magic on the Nile*."

"Wow! We're in Egypt." Grace gave Cuddle an excited squeeze. "Let's go and look at the old pyramid. Maybe we'll find some mummies!"

"Grace," Olivia said, her eyes bright, "does that pyramid look old to you?"

Grace tilted her head and stared at its polished white surface. The profile of the sphinx next to it was crisp and without a single chip. She gasped. "It's brand new. But that means . . ."

". . . we're in *ancient* Egypt!" Olivia finished.

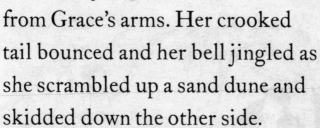

Cuddle jumped from Grace's arms. Her crooked tail bounced and her bell jingled as she scrambled up a sand dune and skidded down the other side.

"Cuddle, come back!" Grace called.

The girls raced after her. The kitten was scampering towards a group of purple-and-blue tents under a clump of palm trees. A young girl about their age emerged from one of the tents. She was wearing a white linen dress with a wide gold necklace. Her hair was long and black and on her wrist was a bracelet shaped like a snake.

She gave a cry as Cuddle jumped into her arms.

"Is this your kitten?" she asked the girls with a smile. "She's beautiful."

"Her name's Cuddle," Olivia said. "I'm Olivia, and this is Grace."

The girl handed Cuddle to Grace.

"I am Beset," she said. She looked at Olivia's denim skirt and Grace's combat trousers. "Do you come from a land far away?"

Grace and Olivia glanced at each other. "That's one way of putting it," Grace replied.

"Welcome, Grace and Olivia," Beset said. "You must be here for the celebration." A frown spread over her face. "But I am afraid it may already be ruined."

"Oh no!" Olivia exclaimed.

"The guest of honour ... she is

missing," Beset explained.

"That's terrible. Maybe we can help you find her. " Grace scanned the landscape. "She should be easy to spot in all this sand."

"What does she look like?" Olivia asked.

"She is as black as night and has a fine silky coat," Beset said.

Olivia pictured a beautiful woman in the expensive sort of coat she'd seen movie stars wear. "It seems too hot for a coat," she said.

"Cleo is like your kitten – she does not mind the heat," Beset said, giving Cuddle a scratch behind the ears. The little kitten wriggled happily in

Grace's arms.

"The guest of honour is a cat?" Grace said in surprise. Beset nodded.

"Cleo is the Pharaoh's kitten. He is hosting a banquet in her honour."

"Who is the Pharaoh?" Olivia asked.

"The Pharaoh is the king of all of Egypt," Beset replied. She looked even more worried. "If I do not find Cleo soon, the Pharaoh will be sad, and I will be in big trouble."

Chapter Four
Cuddle Leads the Way

"Don't worry, Beset," Grace said.
"We'll help you find Cleo."

"Thank you!" Beset said.

"Why are you having a party for
a cat?" Olivia asked, trying not to
giggle.

"Cats are very important to us,"
Beset said. "We even have a special
goddess to protect them."

Cuddle hopped down on to the sand. "Miaow!" The kitten rubbed against Beset's sandals, then darted off towards the pyramid.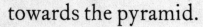

"Cuddle!" Grace called. "Come here!" The kitten stopped and looked back, but then she mewed at the girls and ran off again. The pink pads on her paws flashed as she bounded across the sand.

"I think she wants us to follow her," Olivia said.

They ran after the little kitten, who by now was almost at the pyramid.

Palm trees were planted at each
of the pyramid's four corners, their
green leaves dancing in the sunshine.
Cuddle's bell jingled as she skidded
to the far side of the pyramid. The
girls followed – but the kitten had
disappeared.

"Oh my," Beset said. "Now we will
have to find two missing kittens."

Grace crouched down in the sand.
"Look at this." Olivia and Beset
peered over her shoulder at two sets
of tiny paw prints.

"They must belong to Cuddle
and Cleo. We can follow them to see
where they've got to."

The paw prints wound through
the sand and stopped at a white stone
in the base of the pyramid. Pictures
were engraved in the stone.

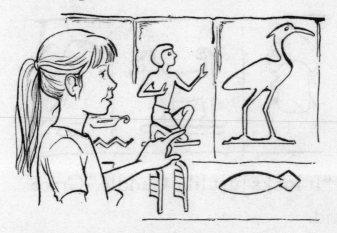

"I like that one," Grace said,
pointing to a bird with long legs.

"They're a special kind of picture,"
Beset explained. "They tell a story.
We call them hieroglyphs."

Suddenly, Olivia gave a shout

53

of surprise. "Hey, look at this hieroglyph."

It was a cat with a curly kink in its tail.

"It looks just like Cuddle," Grace said.

Beset ran her fingers over the cat hieroglyph. The stone wobbled slightly. "Did you see that?" she said. "Maybe this is a secret way into the pyramid."

The three girls placed their hands

on the cat hieroglyph and pushed.

With a rumble, the stone slid inside the pyramid.

Grace gasped. "It's a secret passageway!"

Chapter Five
The Twisty-Turny Maze

Grace crawled through the dusty passageway on her hands and knees. At the end was a dark hole in the floor.

She peered down – it was a narrow shaft. Her heart thumped as she swung her legs over the edge of the hole and let herself fall. She landed in a long, wide corridor with flaming torches flickering on the walls. The air was hot and sticky.

Beset climbed after her, followed by Olivia.

"Yuck," Olivia muttered, pausing to brush the thick dust from her skirt.

Beset walked ahead, her snake bracelet glinting in the torchlight. "There are many, many corridors," she said. "Cuddle and Cleo could be anywhere." She shook her head. "We will never find them in time. The Pharaoh will be very unhappy if Cleo does not come to her own celebration."

"Don't worry. I'm sure we can find them in time," Grace said as she and Olivia hurried after Beset.

Passages led off in all directions, their entrances casting shadows on the smooth yellow floor.

Olivia twisted one of her curls round her finger. It was damp from the warm air. "How do we decide where to look first?" she asked.

Beset frowned. "The men who build the pyramids hide riddles and games inside them – like the secret passageway. Maybe we need to use a riddle to find the way."

Grace began to chant, moving her finger from one corridor to the next with each word. "Eeny, teeny, tiny cat – can you tell me where she's at? Strokes and snuggles, she loves all that,

eeny, teeny, tiny cat." On the last word
she was pointing towards a corridor
on the right. "Let's try that way."

The girls walked down the
corridor, calling the two kittens'
names. It was lined with tall ceramic
jars. The lid of each was shaped like
a bird's head with jewelled eyes that
twinkled as the girls passed. The
corridor twisted round a corner – and

finished at a blank wall.

"It's a dead end," Grace said with a groan.

Disappointed, they wound their way back – and saw a little kitten curled up on the floor where they had started.

"Cuddle!" Olivia cried.

Cuddle rolled on to her back and stretched her paws towards the girls. Grace tickled her tummy and Cuddle purred loudly.

"We've found one kitten," Beset said. "But now we must find Cleo."

Grace said her rhyme again, and this time they went down a corridor on the left. Cuddle sat on Olivia's

shoulder, her head poking through
Olivia's curls.

The corridor swung left, then right,
then left again, winding backwards
and forwards until the girls had no
idea which direction they had come
from. They came to a stop by a tall
statue of a bird with a hooked beak.

"This place is a maze," Olivia said.

"Miaow."

"That's not a real bird, Cuddle!" Grace said. "It's just – "

Olivia put her finger to her lips.

"Miaow."

"That's not Cuddle miaowing," Olivia said. "It's coming from far away."

Beset clapped her hands in delight. "It must be Cleo!"

Chapter Six
All in the Dark

Cuddle leapt from Olivia's shoulder in a flurry of black-and-white fur. Her bell jingled as she scurried along the corridor, her crooked tail twitching behind her.

"Maybe she knows where Cleo is," Olivia said. She grabbed Grace and Beset's hands and they raced after her. The kitten led them down winding corridors and into a large chamber.

"Wow!" Grace said.

The ceiling above them was higher than the roof of her new house. Torches glowed in the branches of palm trees made of gold.

Whoosh! A gust of warm wind swept through the chamber. It blew out the torches, leaving them in complete darkness. The girls cried out in surprise.

Grace huddled next to Olivia. "I don't like the dark much," Grace whispered. Her hands shaking, she reached in the pockets of her combat trousers. She felt elastic bands, foil sweet wrappers and a stick of chewing gum, before pulling out the shiny blue penlight she always carried. Flicking it on, she circled the narrow beam of light around the room.

"I have never seen such a torch before," Beset said. "Is it magical?"

"It's like the ones on the walls, but you can turn it on and off," Grace explained.

Cuddle's bell jingled and Grace trained the beam on her as the kitten disappeared into the darkness.

The girls followed, Grace lighting their way as best she could.

Cuddle stopped by a stone door. Grace moved the penlight over it. The door was covered in carvings of cats, of all shapes and sizes: playing with string, chasing their tails and rolling around.

"I see what you mean, Beset," Olivia said. "Egyptians really do love cats!"

Cuddle mewed and scrabbled against the door with her paws.

"Is Cleo in there?" Beset asked.

"Only one way to find out," Grace

replied.

The girls pushed against the door. It was stiff, and made a grinding noise as it opened a little.

Grace poked her head through the gap. She flashed the penlight around, glimpsing enormous legs, jagged teeth – and a pair of massive eyes staring straight at her.

"It's a monster!" she cried.

Chapter Seven
Cat Chase

Beset took the penlight from Grace,
her shaking hands making the beam
of light wobble. She slowly peeked
round the door – and started to
laugh.

"It is just a statue," she said.

Grace and Olivia followed her into
the room. Beset trained the light on
a wooden statue, twice as tall as a

man. It had a human body and a head like a dog's. Its eyes were made from glittering emeralds.

"What kind of creature is it?" Grace asked.

"That is not a creature," Beset explained. "It is Anubis – one of our gods. He looks after people when they die."

Jingle jangle jingle. Cuddle came in behind them. Beset shone the light on the little kitten and she wiggled her whiskers.

The girls gasped as a torch on the wall burst into flame, then another, and another, until the room was bathed in light.

"Did Cuddle do that?" Beset asked, her eyes wide.

Grace tickled the kitten's ears.

"I wouldn't be surprised. She brought us here, after all."

"Cuddle," Olivia said, giving the kitten a kiss on the head, "is clever as well as cute!"

In the light the girls could see that the statue of Anubis was surrounded by glittering treasures. A golden sphinx – like the one they had seen outside, only much, much smaller –

jugs stood next to thick cushions.

Olivia knelt by a turquoise chest brimming over with necklaces, bracelets and jewels.

Grace ran her hand over the smooth
head of a cat carved from green stone.
There were lots of cat statues sitting
neatly in lines, some crouched on
their haunches, one washing its fur
with a flickering pink tongue...

Hold on, that statue was moving!

"Beset – I think I've found Cleo," Grace said.

Beset gave a cry of delight. But Cleo darted away; a streak of short black fur and bright blue eyes.

Cuddle sprang on to the head of the golden sphinx. "Miaow!"

"Miaow!" Cleo replied. She bounded out from behind Anubis, pranced up the sphinx's back and sat next to Cuddle. Her black fur was covered in dust.

81

"I think Cleo would rather play with Cuddle than go to the celebration," Grace said.

Beset sat down with a sigh. "You are correct. Cleo has many celebrations to attend. However, I do not think she enjoys them. Being the Pharaoh's kitten does not leave much time for playing."

Olivia tugged on one of her curls, her lips pursed together thoughtfully. "Maybe we could make it more fun for her," she said.

"That would be wonderful," Beset said. "But how?"

"We can make her a new toy," Grace said, opening the pockets of her combat trousers. She tipped shiny foil, a lolly stick, a seashell, garden twine and a drinking straw on to the floor. Olivia emptied lip balm, a hairbrush and some sparkly hairgrips from her bag.

Cuddle jumped down from the sphinx and bounded over. Cleo trotted to sit beside her, sniffing the heap of objects.

Beset caught Cleo at last, and nuzzled the top of her furry head. "You are very messy," she said. "You cannot go to the celebration like this."

Olivia picked up her hairbrush from the pile. "No problem. I'll make her look fit for a Pharaoh. It's kitten makeover time!"

Beset put Cleo in Olivia's lap, and Olivia brushed the dust off her fur.

Cuddle gave her a lick too, and soon Cleo's coat was gleaming.

"She looks glorious." Beset reached into the pocket of her gown and drew out a collar. It was studded with glittering red jewels, each shaped like a tiny paw print.

"This is Cleo's special celebration collar," she said, slipping it over the kitten's head.

"It's beautiful," Olivia said.

"Here," called Grace. She was holding the lolly stick. The twine was tied to the top, and knotted along its length were all the other objects. Right at the end were Olivia's sparkly hairgrips.

Grace shook the stick and the objects jiggled.

"Miaow!" Cleo pounced on the twine, making the girls laugh.

"She can play with her new toy during the celebration," Olivia said. "That's brilliant, Grace."

"Thank you both," Beset said, though she still looked worried. "But how will we make it to the celebration in time if we can't find our way back out of the pyramid?"

Chapter Eight
Join the Parade

Olivia and Grace looked at each other. "Cuddle brought us here . . ." Olivia began.

". . . she'll show us the way out," Grace finished.

The black-and-white kitten raced back through the pyramid. Cleo followed her, the toy in her mouth, with the girls behind.

As Cuddle sprinted past, each of
the torches on the walls magically
relit, lighting their way.

They crawled out through the
secret passageway, tumbling over
each other on to the sand.

Somewhere on the other side of the
pyramid, the air rang with the sounds

of cheering and clapping.

"What's happening?" Grace
wondered, climbing to her feet.

"The celebration is about to start,"
Beset said. "We must hurry!" She led
the girls round the pyramid.

A parade of people were dancing across the sand, their white robes and jewelled necklaces shimmering in the sun. They were heading towards the purple and blue tents.

The girls hurried to the front of the parade. Four attendants were carrying an enormous cushion, as blue as Cleo's eyes. Beset placed Cleo in the middle of it, and the crowd cheered. The little black kitten rolled around, batting the toy with her paws.

Olivia and Grace joined the dancing crowd, laughing as they took it in turns to twirl Cuddle around.

Beset and Cleo led the parade into

the largest tent. The tent was filled
with tables laden with fruit and
sugared pastries, and in the centre
was a beautiful golden throne.

A man was sitting on it, wearing a
tall red-and-white crown.

"He must be the Pharaoh,"
whispered Grace, hugging Cuddle
to her.

Beset placed Cleo at the Pharaoh's feet. The kitten rubbed against his jewelled sandals, and Beset bowed low to the ground. Grace and Olivia did the same. Cuddle sprang from Grace's arms. She jumped on to the arm of the golden throne and seemed to bow to the Pharaoh too.

Olivia held her breath. Would the Pharaoh be cross?

But he smiled and stroked Cuddle all the way from her nose to the curly tip of her tail. "Cats are very special," he said. "Some might say magical. Thank you for returning Cleo to me."

When the girls bowed again,
Cuddle leapt down from the throne,
pushing through the crowd.

"Goodbye, Pharaoh! Goodbye,
Beset!" the girls called, following
Cuddle out of the tent and back into
the heat of the desert.

Olivia gazed around at the vast
sandy landscape.

She suddenly missed Catterton's neat rows of houses and leafy gardens filled with flowers.

"We found Cleo, but now we're the ones who are lost," she said. "How will we ever find our way home?"

As if answering, the little kitten rubbed against the girls' legs, weaving round their feet in looping figures of eight.

Her purr grew louder, and the sand, the pyramid, the sphinx and the parade became a whirl of colour.

"Cuddle's taking us home," Grace called. The girls held hands tightly and closed their eyes as ancient Egypt melted away . . .

When Olivia opened her eyes, they were back in Grace's garden. The apple tree, the cardboard boxes, the sandpit – everything seemed exactly the same.

Grace scratched her head. "What just happened? Did Cuddle really take us to ancient Egypt?"

"I think so," Olivia said, "but now I can't see her anywhere."

Jingle jangle jingle.

The girls spun round. Cuddle was walking along the top of the fence that separated their two gardens. She flicked her crooked tail and lifted her little black paw in what looked like a wave.

Then, in a haze of sparkles, she disappeared.

"Goodbye, Cuddle!" Grace said. "Do you think we'll see her again?"

"I hope so," Olivia replied with a smile. "Maybe she'll take us on another adventure."

"You know," Grace said, her eyes shining, "I think I'm going to love living here."

Can't wait to find out
what Cuddle will do next?
Then read on! Here is the first chapter
from Cuddle's second adventure,
SUPERSTAR DREAMS . . .

Superstar Dreams

A breeze rippled through the cherry tree, making its pink blossom dance. Grace's combat trousers and T-shirt were scattered with sweet-smelling petals.

"It's like being in a blossomy snowstorm," she called down to Olivia. "Climb up and see."

"I've never climbed a tree before,"

Olivia said, twirling one of her curls round and round a finger.

The girls were in Olivia's back garden. Grace was sitting in the cherry tree, while Olivia stood beside the trunk. From her perch, Grace could see her own back garden next door. The roofs of the houses that lined their street were still damp from a recent rain shower. The sky over Catterton was dark grey.

"Let's see if you can get up here before it rains again," Grace said. "I'll help you."

"All right," Olivia said. "Here goes." Stretching up on to the tips of her blue sandals, she grabbed the lowest branch.

"That's it," Grace said. "Now wrap your legs round the trunk and hold the next branch."

Olivia could see Grace's smiling face through the leaves, framed by her shiny blonde hair. She stretched up for the branch, but her fingers slid over a patch of moss. With a shriek, she tumbled to the ground.

Grace scrambled down after her. "Are you okay?"

Olivia was lying face up, her black curls fanned out on the ground. "I'm fine," she said, smiling. "Now do you believe I can't climb trees?"

Grace pulled Olivia to her feet.

"You just need to practise. Then you'll be able to climb like a cat!"

At that moment, a sunbeam pushed its way through the clouds, scattering golden rays.

Olivia clapped her hands. "Oh! Do you think Cuddle's on her way?"

Cuddle was a cute kitten who had recently appeared in a beam of sunlight and taken the girls on a magical adventure.

Jingle jangle jingle.

"That's Cuddle's bell!" Grace cried.

The sunbeam shone on Olivia's bike, which was propped up against the back of the house. A pink basket was fixed to the handlebars. It

wiggled and jiggled, and Cuddle's
black-and-white face poked out.
Her green eyes sparkled in the sun.

"Hello, Cuddle!" both girls cried.

Olivia grinned. "The sunbeam
looks like a spotlight. Cuddle's
a movie star."

The kitten's bell jingled as she
sprang on to the bike's saddle. With
a swish of her crooked tail, she leapt
into Grace's arms and mewed loudly,
as if greeting her friends.

Grace hugged the kitten tightly.

"You certainly live up to your name,
don't you, Cuddle?" she said.

Purrrrrrrr, went Cuddle. She
sounded like a tiny rumble of thunder.

The girls' skin tingled, as if Cuddle's whiskers were tickling them. Cuddle's purr grew louder and louder, and the girls started to giggle. They leaned in to each other, the little kitten cradled between them.

Now they knew what would happen next – kitten magic! As Cuddle's purr rumbled on, the garden and the cherry tree faded away ...

***

To find out what happens next,

get your copy of

Superstar Dreams today!

Cuddle
★ the cutest kitten ★

Superstar Dreams

Is Chloe brave enough
to perform on stage?

Cuddle uses her
magic to take
Olivia and Grace
backstage at a
talent show. Can
the girls persuade
talented Chloe
to audition even
though she's lost
her lucky charm?

Find out in SUPERSTAR DREAMS...

Cuddle
★ the cutest kitten ★

Princess Party Sleepover

Who wants to be a princess?

Princess Victoria doesn't. She'd much rather be wearing old clothes and climbing trees. Can Cuddle, Olivia and Grace convince her that being a princess can be fun in time for the royal ball?

Find out in PRINCESS PARTY SLEEPOVER...

Cuddle

★ the cutest kitten ★

School of Spells

Join Cuddle, Grace and Olivia on
a magical school adventure!

Cuddle takes the
girls to a school
with a difference
– the pupils are
enchanted creatures
and the lessons are
magical! But will
they be able to help
a shy unicorn make
some friends?

Find out in SCHOOL OF SPELLS...

Puddle the naughtiest puppy

If you like Cuddle the Cutest Kitten
you'll love Puddle the Naughtiest Puppy!

Puddle is a mischievous puppy who
appears every time it rains. He only has
to jump into a puddle to take cousins
Ruby and Harry on a series of amazing
magical adventures.

Why not begin your Puddle
collection today?

Helping cats with Cats Protection

Grace, Olivia and Cuddle have lots of fun on their adventures together, but real cats and kittens need a lot of looking after. That's why our friends at Cats Protection are going to be joining us in each book to talk about everything a cat needs for a happy home life.

The most important part of Cats Protection's work is finding new homes for unwanted and abandoned cats and kittens. They spend lots of time making sure that each cat is ready for a new home, and always try to match the right cat with the right owner!

Always remember: Cuddle is a magical kitten, while real cats and kittens are living animals who need a lot of care, love and attention.

Why do cats come to Cats Protection?

- When an elderly owner dies and there is no one else to look after the cat
- When a cat has kittens and the owner can't look after them
- When cats are saved from unsafe places and cruel treatment
- When people move house and can no longer keep their cat
- When a cat is found wandering the streets and has no owner

Cats Protection staff and volunteers work to make sure no cats are treated badly or left to stray on the street. They never put a healthy cat to sleep.

Congratulations – now you know why cats might need help from Cats Protection. Next time, find out what you need when you take a cat home.

Cats Protection is the UK's leading feline welfare charity. Cats Protection has been helping cats since 1927 and each year they help more than 215,000 cats and kittens, giving them the chance of a better life.

To find out more, please go to: www.cats.org.uk
For more cool cat facts, games and downloads, visit www.cats.org.uk/cats-for-kids

Jigsaw Jumble

Look carefully at the picture of
Olivia, Grace and Beset opposite.
It has several pieces missing. Can you
work out where each jigsaw piece
should go?

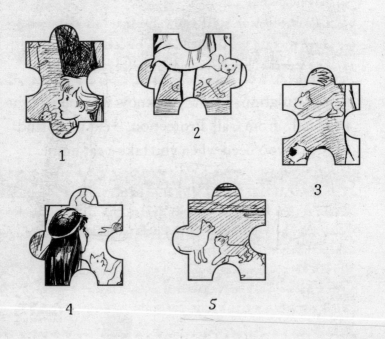

Answers at the end of the book

Pyramid Puzzle

Look at the strange words below.
Can you unscramble each one to make
the name of something the girls saw in
ancient Egypt? Then match each one
to a picture.

1. ramypid

2. pinxsh

3. Paharoh

4. Abnusi

5. rophglyies

A

B

C

D

E

Answers at the end of the book

Cuddle
★ the cutest kitten ★

To find out more about the adorable
Cuddle and her magical adventures, visit

www.ladybird.com/cuddlethekitten

Read hints and tips from Cats Protection
on how to look after your own cat,
plus download lots of fun activities.

Find more fantastic Ladybird titles at
www.ladybird.com

Answers to Cuddle Puzzles:
Jigsaw Jumble: 1 – C, 2 – D, 3 – E, 4 – B, 5 – A
Pyramid Puzzle: 1: pyramid – A, 2: sphinx – B, 3: Pharaoh – E,
4: Anubis – D, 5: hieroglyphs – C